For Jerry — J.D.

For Dartington Playgroup — N.S.

First published 2012 by Macmillan Children's Books
a division of Macmillan Publishers Limited
20 New Wharf Road, London N1 9RR
Basingstoke and Oxford
Associated companies throughout the world
www.panmacmillan.com
ISBN: 978-0-330-51228-2
Text copyright © Julia Donaldson 2012
Illustrations copyright © Nick Sharratt 2012

3 5 7 9 8 6 4 2

A CIP catalogue record for this book is available from the British Library.
Printed in China

Written by

Julia Donaldson

Illustrated by

Nick Sharratt

Goat Goes To Playgroup

To Gabe,
Have "big fun"
at school
Love Aunt Sue
?
Uncle
Steve

MACMILLAN CHILDREN'S BOOKS

Playgroup has begun.

Time to have some fun.

...t hangs up her coat.

Don't be silly, Goat!

Squirrel likes the sand.

Goat has joined a band.

A pot of paint for Weasel.

Goat knocks down an easel.

Dog puts on a dress.

Goat is in a mess.

A bunch of grapes for Goose.

Goat has spilt his juice.

Monkey has a cuddle.

Goat is in a puddle.

Mouse is sowing seeds.

Goat pulls up the weeds.

Squirrel likes to sing.

Goat falls off the swing.

Badger reads a book.

Goat decides to cook.

Now it's circle time.

Goat would rather climb.

Home time – look who's come!

Can you see Goat's mum?